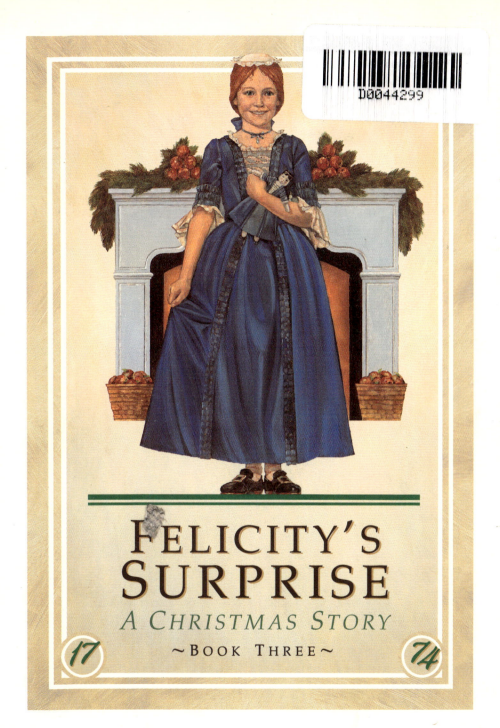

FELICITY'S SURPRISE

A CHRISTMAS STORY

~BOOK THREE~

17 *74*

THE AMERICAN GIRLS COLLECTION®

FELICITY'S SURPRISE
A CHRISTMAS STORY
BY VALERIE TRIPP

Felicity is invited to a dancing lesson at the elegant Governor's Palace, the most wonderful honor she can imagine. Mother promises to make a beautiful new gown for her, just like the one shown on the fashion doll at the milliner's shop. As the splendid event draws near, Mother becomes dreadfully ill. Felicity spends all her days caring for her, sadly accepting that there will be no new gown and no chance to go to the Palace. No chance, that is, until a glorious surprise reminds her that Christmastide is a time when hopes and dreams do come true.

PRESENTS

THE AMERICAN GIRLS COLLECTION ®

17 74

MEET FELICITY · An American Girl
FELICITY LEARNS A LESSON · A School Story
FELICITY'S SURPRISE · A Christmas Story

18 54

MEET KIRSTEN · An American Girl
KIRSTEN LEARNS A LESSON · A School Story
KIRSTEN'S SURPRISE · A Christmas Story
HAPPY BIRTHDAY, KIRSTEN! · A Springtime Story
KIRSTEN SAVES THE DAY · A Summer Story
CHANGES FOR KIRSTEN · A Winter Story

19 04

MEET SAMANTHA · An American Girl
SAMANTHA LEARNS A LESSON · A School Story
SAMANTHA'S SURPRISE · A Christmas Story
HAPPY BIRTHDAY, SAMANTHA! · A Springtime Story
SAMANTHA SAVES THE DAY · A Summer Story
CHANGES FOR SAMANTHA · A Winter Story

19 44

MEET MOLLY · An American Girl
MOLLY LEARNS A LESSON · A School Story
MOLLY'S SURPRISE · A Christmas Story
HAPPY BIRTHDAY, MOLLY! · A Springtime Story
MOLLY SAVES THE DAY · A Summer Story
CHANGES FOR MOLLY · A Winter Story

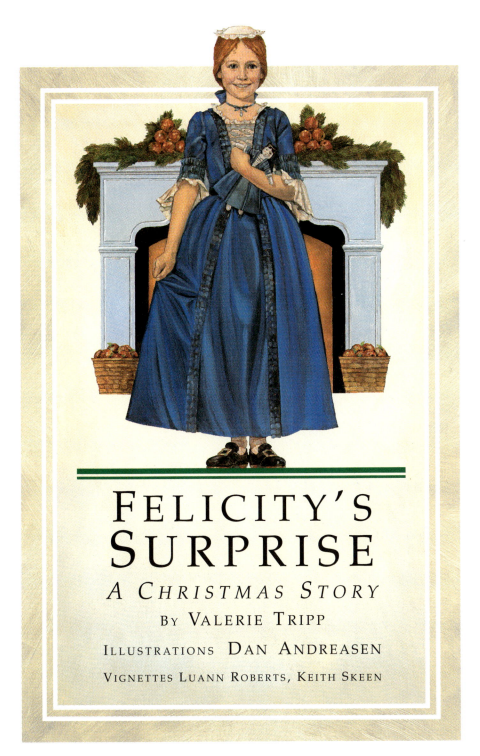

FELICITY'S SURPRISE

A CHRISTMAS STORY

BY VALERIE TRIPP

ILLUSTRATIONS DAN ANDREASEN

VIGNETTES LUANN ROBERTS, KEITH SKEEN

PLEASANT COMPANY

PICTURE CREDITS
The following individuals and organizations have generously given
permission to reprint illustrations contained in "Looking Back":
pp. 64-65—Colonial Williamsburg Foundation; The Shrine to Music Museum at the
University of South Dakota; *The End of the Hunt,* Anonymous American, National Gallery
of Art, Washington, Gift of Edgar William and Bernice Chrysler Garbisch; pp. 66-67—
Colonial Williamsburg Foundation (large doll); Hammond-Harwood House Association,
Annapolis, Maryland; The New-York Historical Society, N.Y.C.; pp. 68-69—Courtesy,
Winterthur Museum; Colonial Williamsburg Foundation; Courtesy, Winterthur Museum.

Edited by Carolyn Hardesty
Designed by Myland McRevey and Michael Victor

Art Directed by Kathleen A. Brown

Library of Congress Cataloging-in-Publication Data

Tripp, Valerie, 1951-
Felicity's surprise : a Christmas story / by Valerie Tripp ; illustrations, Dan Andreasen ;
vignettes, Luann Roberts, Keith Skeen.

p. cm. — (The American girls collection)
Summary: Christmas in Williamsburg means a dancing party at the Governor's Palace for
Felicity, but her mother becomes very ill and cannot finish the special blue gown.

ISBN 1-56247-009-4 — ISBN 1-56247-010-8 (pbk.)
[1. Christmas—Fiction. 2. Williamsburg (Va.)—Fiction.
3. Virginia—Social life and customs—Colonial period, ca. 1600-1775—Fiction.
4. Friendship—Fiction.]
I. Andreasen, Dan, ill. II. Title. III. Series.
PZ7.T7363Fel 1991 [Fic]—dc20 91-20704 CIP AC

TO ALICE MARTIN TRIPP

TABLE OF CONTENTS

FELICITY'S FAMILY
AND FRIENDS

FATHER

Felicity's father, who owns one of the general stores in Williamsburg.

MOTHER

Felicity's mother, who takes care of her family with love and pride.

FELICITY

A spunky, spritely colonial girl, growing up just before the American Revolution in 1774.

NAN

Felicity's sweet and sensible sister, who is six years old.

WILLIAM

Felicity's almost-three brother, who likes mischief and mud puddles.

BEN DAVIDSON
A quiet apprentice living with the Merrimans while learning to work in Father's store.

MISS MANDERLY
Felicity's teacher— a gracious gentlewoman.

ELIZABETH COLE
Felicity's best friend is new to the colonies and admires Felicity.

ANNABELLE COLE
Elizabeth's snobby older sister who thinks everything in England is better.

ROSE
The cook and maidservant at the Merrimans'.

AN INVITATION TO THE PALACE

Felicity ran along the frozen path as if she were running toward Christmas. Then quick! She turned sideways and slid, slick as a fish, across a smooth stretch of ice. "Try sliding!" she called back to her sister Nan. "It's *fast!* I'm going to do it again!"

Nan grinned but shook her head. "We shouldn't slide, Lissie. It isn't proper," she said. "And anyway, you know we promised Mother we wouldn't play. We said we'd come straight home after we cut enough holly to fill our baskets."

"Very well," said Felicity cheerfully. She knew Nan was right, as usual. Besides, she had already spotted more clear patches of ice ahead. So she ran

1

and slid, ran and slid, while Nan trotted along behind, carefully picking up the holly sprigs that fell out of Felicity's basket.

"Mother! William!" called Felicity as she and Nan burst into the house. "Come see the holly we've cut. 'Tis ever so full of berries!"

Mrs. Merriman and little William hurried to greet the girls.

"Look at all the holly!" said William. "A lot and a lot!"

Mrs. Merriman smiled. "My two Christmas sprites!" she said. "You *have* done a fine job. The holly is perfect. Now I can work Christmas magic on the house. But look at you! Your noses are as red and cold as the holly berries.

"Go sit yourselves by the fire. Lissie, take your shoes off first. Don't track that muddy slush into the parlor." She scooped up William with one arm and the two holly baskets with the other. "Later, you can help me decorate. It will be a fine surprise for your father and Ben."

Just then, they heard polite knocking on the door. "Oh, Lissie," said Mrs. Merriman. "My hands are full. Do please answer the door."

"Yes, Mother," said Felicity. The floor was slippery, and she slid a little as she hurried to the door. When she opened it, she stepped back in surprise. "Goodness!" she gasped.

There stood a very elegantly dressed man. He bowed to Mrs. Merriman. "Good day, madam," he said. "Do I have the honor of addressing the wife of Mr. Edward Merriman?" Felicity's mother nodded, and the man held out a letter. "This is for you, madam," he said.

Mrs. Merriman quickly put William and the holly baskets down and took the letter. "Thank you," she said as the man left. "Good day to you."

Felicity, Nan, and William crowded close to Mother as she untied the red ribbon and opened the letter. "Why, Lissie!" she exclaimed. "It is from Lady Dunmore, the royal governor's wife. It's an invitation for *you*."

"Me?" gasped Felicity.

"Just listen," said Mrs. Merriman. She cleared her throat and read the invitation. "Lady Dunmore presents her compliments to Mrs. Merriman and requests the favor of her daughter Felicity's

attendance at a dancing lesson at the Palace on
Saturday, January seven at four o'clock."

"Oooh, Lissie!" sighed Nan. "You are so lucky!"

Mother handed the invitation to Felicity. She
read it, but she could hardly believe the message
written in curlicues and fancy script. *She* was
invited to the royal Governor's Palace. The Palace
was the fanciest, most *elegant* place in Williamsburg.
Many times she'd peeked through the iron gates in
the high brick wall around it. And now she was
invited to come inside, as a guest! Felicity was
speechless. The room was so quiet, they all jumped

when they heard more knocking at the door.

"Whatever now?" laughed Mrs. Merriman. "I shouldn't be surprised if it's King George himself!"

But it was Felicity's friend, Elizabeth, waving an invitation just like Felicity's. "Oh, you got yours, too!" she exclaimed. Her brown eyes were bright with excitement. "Isn't it wonderful? Both of us invited to the Palace! Won't it be grand? A dance lesson isn't like a school lesson. There will be music, and lovely food, and everyone wearing beautiful clothes. This dance lesson will be almost like a ball!"

"A ball!" said Nan, wide-eyed.

Elizabeth rattled on, "My mother says our teacher, Miss Manderly, arranged for us to be invited. Miss Manderly knows the dancing master who teaches the governor's children. She asked him to invite you and me and my sister Annabelle. Aren't you excited?"

"Yes!" laughed Felicity. "I think I must be in a dream."

"The cold will wake you from your dream," smiled Mrs. Merriman. "Put your shoes back on, Lissie. Go to the store and show the invitation to your father. You must ask his permission to go to the dancing lesson. Hurry now."

Felicity pulled her shoes back on. "Can you come to the store with me, Elizabeth?" she asked.

"No, I'd best not," Elizabeth answered. "My mother doesn't like me to be out in the cold. She's certain I'll catch a fever." The two girls shared a look that said, *Aren't mothers silly, always worried about fevers and such?* Then Elizabeth left for home.

Felicity gave no thought to the cold as she stepped out into the twilight. There was a happy feeling in the city of Williamsburg that evening. Windows in many of the houses and shops were trimmed inside with holiday greenery as if they were dressed up for a special occasion. Some wore

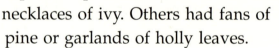

necklaces of ivy. Others had fans of pine or garlands of holly leaves.

Christmastide was Felicity's favorite time of year. It was the season of celebrations, pretty decorations, and many visitors. And this Christmas promised to be the most wonderful ever. This Christmas Felicity was invited to the Palace! Felicity held her invitation safe under her cloak and hurried toward her father's store.

The store was empty of customers, though it was not yet closing time. In November, Mr. Merriman had stopped selling tea in his store to show that he was against the tax the king had put on tea. Since then, the store was never very busy. People who agreed with the king had stopped shopping there. Felicity stepped into the shadowy store lit by a few flickering candles. She called out, "Hello! Hello!"

"Hello, yourself!" answered a cheery voice. It was Ben, Mr. Merriman's apprentice. He was up on a ladder, dusting high shelves. He grinned down at Felicity. "This is a fine surprise," he said. "Have you come for a whistling lesson?"

"Not this time," laughed Felicity. "Where's Father?"

"In his counting room," said Ben. "What's happened?"

"Oh, nothing!" said Felicity airily. "Only the very finest thing ever in the world!"

"And what might that be?" laughed Ben.

But Felicity did not answer him, because she saw her father coming. "Father! Look!" she cried as she rushed toward him, waving the invitation. "Elizabeth and Annabelle and I have been invited to the Palace!"

"To the Palace?" Mr. Merriman exclaimed. He opened the invitation and held it near the candlelight. Ben climbed down the ladder and came to take a look, too.

"May I go, Father? Elizabeth says it will be almost like a ball!" said Felicity, placing her hand on his arm. "Oh, please say I can go!"

"Well, I . . ." her father began.

"Lissie!" Ben burst out before Mr. Merriman could finish. "How can you even *consider* it? How could you possibly go to the Governor's Palace? How could you smile at the governor and drink his punch as if you're the best of friends? How *could* you?"

"I'm not angry at the governor," Felicity said hotly.

"You should be!" said Ben. "You know Governor Dunmore represents the king here in Virginia. You know the king and the governor have treated us colonists badly!"

"Well," said Felicity. "I suppose so, but . . ."

"Lissie!" Ben burst out. "How could you possibly go to the Governor's Palace?"

Ben didn't listen. "If you go to this dance lesson, you'll be surrounded by Loyalists," he said. "You'll be dancing with children of the very same people who have snubbed us and refused to shop at your father's store ever since we stopped selling tea." Ben shook his head. "Don't you see, Lissie? You can't go. You *can't.*"

Felicity felt plunged in gloom. She understood everything Ben was saying, but she still wanted to go to the dance lesson. She looked at her father. *"Is it wrong for me to go to the Palace, Father?"* she asked.

Mr. Merriman looked down into Felicity's sad face. "Lissie, my dear," he said. "I think it is wrong when adults' arguments make children unhappy. The invitation is kind. The governor and his lady are parents, just as I am. They want their children to be happy, especially at Christmastide. Christmas is not the time for anger. It is the time for friendliness and good spirit and merriment, too."

"So you say she should go, sir?" asked Ben. He sounded surprised.

"Indeed, yes. I *do* think Felicity should go to the Governor's Palace," answered Mr. Merriman. "And she should dance with the governor's children and their friends. Because if our children can dance together, then perhaps we adults can settle our differences without fighting."

Felicity smiled at her father. "Oh, thank you, Father," she said. "I did so hope you would say I could go."

Mr. Merriman smiled, too. "Christmas is the time our hopes for peace and happiness should come true," he said.

Felicity looked at Ben. She hoped Father had made him think that it was right for her to go to the dance lesson. But Ben was frowning. Felicity knew she had disappointed him. "Ben," she began, "It's *Christmas* . . ."

Ben turned sharply and walked away, out of the candlelight.

SUGAR CAKES AND CHRISTMAS HOPES

Cheerful sunlight shone through the windows into the kitchen. Felicity and Elizabeth were having a merry, messy time baking Shrewsbury cakes. Elizabeth was beating an egg and rose water together in a bowl. Felicity had unwrapped the blue paper from a sugar loaf and was scraping off a cup of sugar.

"Five days till Christmas," said Felicity. "And then thirteen days till we go to the Palace. It seems such a terribly long time to wait."

"Yes!" agreed Elizabeth. She added a pinch of nutmeg to the bowl. "I think about the dance lesson *all* the time."

Felicity spooned the sugar and some butter into

Elizabeth's bowl. "When you lived in England, did you ever go to a dance lesson as fancy as this one will be?" she asked.

"Oh, no!" said Elizabeth. "Never anything as grand as this! Mother says it is such a special occasion, Annabelle and I will ride to the Palace in a carriage. We shall each have a footman to escort us right up to the Palace door. Who will escort you, Lissie?"

"I don't know," said Felicity. "Most likely my father will."

Elizabeth grinned. "I have a fine idea!" she said. "*Ben* could escort you to the Palace. That would make Annabelle green with envy!"

Elizabeth's snobby older sister Annabelle was sweet on Ben. The girls had shared many a giggle over the way Annabelle fluttered her eyelashes at Ben, trying to make him notice her. So Elizabeth looked surprised when Felicity frowned and said sharply, "No! Ben will *not* escort me to the Palace."

"But why not?" asked Elizabeth. "He is your friend."

Felicity thumped the dough hard with the rolling pin. "Ben does not think I should go to the dance lesson at the Palace at all," she said. "He is angry at the governor and the Loyalists. He thinks I should be angry, too."

"Oh," said Elizabeth softly. Elizabeth's parents were Loyalists. Her father was friendly with the governor.

"But my father said the governor and his lady were kind to invite me, and that I should go," said Felicity. "He said Christmas is the time when our hopes for peace and happiness should come true."

"Well, that's a good thing," said Elizabeth. She sounded relieved. "Because it would be terrible if you couldn't go. I wouldn't even *like* the dance lesson if you were not there."

"Don't worry!" said Felicity with a grin. "I'll be there! I promise!" She wiped her floury hands on her apron. "Now, then," she asked, "which cake cutter do you want to use first? The star, the moon, the heart, or the clover?"

"Oh, the star," said Elizabeth. "I want to use the Christmas star first."

That afternoon, Felicity brought a pretty basket of the Shrewsbury cakes she and Elizabeth had made to lessons at Miss Manderly's house.

"Such lovely cakes," said Miss Manderly. "Thank you, Felicity."

"Elizabeth and I made them," said Felicity. "We wanted to thank you for our invitations to the dance lesson. I never dreamed I would be invited to the Palace. 'Tis a great honor."

"I'm glad you are pleased," said Miss Manderly. "I know you young ladies will do honor to your parents and to my instruction."

"Do you suppose we will be presented to the Governor and Lady Dunmore?" asked Elizabeth. "Will we be introduced to them?"

"Perhaps," said Miss Manderly.

"Well," said Annabelle in a snooty voice. "If we *are* introduced, the Governor and Lady Dunmore will know who Elizabeth and I are. They know our father. When they hear our last name, they will know we are from a family of Loyalists."

Governor and Lady Dunmore may know of my father, too, thought Felicity. *When they hear my last name, they will know I am not from a family of Loyalists. Maybe they won't like me.* She felt a little nervous.

"The governor and his lady will care more about your manners than your name," said Miss Manderly. "We must practice making a courtesy so that you will make a good impression if you are introduced."

Miss Manderly had taught the girls to "make a courtesy" in order to show their respect when they met someone important. Now Felicity stood with Annabelle and Elizabeth to practice. Miss Manderly reminded them of the movements.

"Stand with your back straight," said Miss Manderly as she watched them. "Put one foot slightly in front of the other. Your head should be bowed and tilted to the side a bit. Eyes looking down, Annabelle. 'Tis rude to stare boldly. Now sink down. Slowly! And say softly, 'My lord. My lady.' And then rise. Quite good! But Felicity, don't sink so low. Then you will not wobble. You don't want to fall in a heap at the governor's feet!"

"No, Miss Manderly," said Felicity.

"Oh!" tittered Annabelle. "Can you imagine what an embarrassment it would be to fall!" She looked at Felicity out of the corner of her eye. "I have heard that the dance master is very strict," she

*"Slowly," said Miss Manderly. "You don't want to fall in a heap
at the governor's feet."*

17

prattled on. "He struck two girls because they made mistakes in the dance! And once he scolded a young man sharply because his manner was not quite correct."

"That's enough, Annabelle," said Miss Manderly. "You will all dance beautifully, especially if you practice between now and the day of the dance lesson." She sat at the spinet. "Let us begin our dance practice now. Then none of you need worry."

But Felicity *was* worried. She knew she was not good at dancing. And today she was worse than usual. She even stepped on Elizabeth's toe! What if she should

spinet

step on the toe of one of the governor's sons! Soon Felicity was so busy worrying, she lost track of the dance entirely. Elizabeth tried to help by whispering instructions to her.

"Point your toe!" Elizabeth whispered. She counted the steps for Felicity in a soft voice. "Step on one, sink down on two, step three, four, five. Sink down on six. Now backwards!"

But Felicity was red-faced and fussed. She just couldn't get back in step. It seemed like hours before Miss Manderly said dance practice was over and they could all go.

As they were walking home, Felicity said to Elizabeth, "I was so excited about going to the Palace, I forgot the invitation was for a dance lesson. If we were going to run races or ride horses, then I know I would do well. But I am terrible at dancing."

"Silly old Annabelle made you nervous today with all her talk about the strict dance master," Elizabeth said calmly. "You'll do fine at the Palace."

"No I won't!" exclaimed Felicity. She turned to her friend. "Oh, Elizabeth," she said desperately, "I want to go to the dance lesson at the Palace more than anything in the world. But . . . but the truth is, I am afraid."

"Afraid!" said Elizabeth. "Why, Felicity, you're the bravest girl I know!"

Felicity shook her head. "Not this time," she said. "I'm afraid I will look like a fool."

"You will *not* look like a fool," said Elizabeth loyally. "You will look beautiful. I can imagine it. You will make a courtesy perfectly. The governor and his lady will be charmed. And you will dance like a dream. Your gown will be all shiny in the candlelight. Your petticoats will swirl around you. And everyone will say, who is that graceful and elegant young lady?"

Felicity grinned. When Elizabeth described the scene, she could almost see herself looking elegant at the Palace.

"What are you going to wear?" asked Elizabeth. The question brought Felicity back to earth.

"Oh," she said. "I hadn't thought about that. I'll wear my brown silk gown, I suppose."

"The one you wear to church every Sunday?" Elizabeth asked.

"Yes," said Felicity. "It's my best."

"Oh, yes, of course," said Elizabeth quickly. "That gown always looks fine. You will be comfortable, too, because it's not—it's not so awfully fancy. And you are used to wearing it because it is not new."

"Are you going to wear a new gown?" Felicity asked.

"No, no," said Elizabeth. "It's not new. Well, it is new to *me*. It is one of Annabelle's old silk gowns. My mother is making a new stomacher for it and trimming it with new lace."

"It sounds most elegant," said Felicity wistfully.

Elizabeth shrugged as if she wanted Felicity to think she did not care about clothes. "My mother and Annabelle say that Lady Dunmore is the most fashionable lady in all the colonies," she said. "They are making a fuss about the gowns. I don't think clothes are so terribly important."

That is what Elizabeth said, but Felicity could tell she did not really mean it. Felicity knew Elizabeth thought it was very important to wear a wonderful gown to the Palace.

Felicity did not usually pay much attention to clothes. But now she began to think Elizabeth was absolutely right. "If I had a beautiful new gown I wouldn't be nervous," said Felicity. "Then I would dance well. I would not make any mistakes. If I had a new gown, everything would be perfect."

Elizabeth asked, "Do you think you might have one if you asked your mother?"

"I don't think so," Felicity said sadly. "My mother is so busy just now, getting ready for Christmas. And she and my father are worried about money. There hasn't been much business at the store of late."

"Oh," said Elizabeth. She was quiet. Then she said, "Well . . . well, you might just *ask.* Remember what your father said about hopes coming true at Christmastide."

"Perhaps," said Felicity, "perhaps." Felicity thought *asking* for a new gown just now would be selfish. But she could not help *hoping* for one.

—

TIDINGS OF COMFORT AND JOY

The next morning, Mrs. Merriman said, "Felicity, come along with me. I'm going to the apothecary to get medicine for my cough. We can stop by the milliner on the way home. Perhaps we can find some trim or lace to spruce up your brown silk gown for the dance lesson at the Palace. Would you fancy that?"

"Yes, Mother," said Felicity. She tried to sound pleased. But she was thinking, *Even with new trim, I will still look like a little brown field mouse!*

Felicity trailed along with her mother from shop to shop. She was thinking so hard about asking for a new gown, she only half heard the apothecary and her mother chatting.

"Mrs. Merriman," said Mr. Galt, the apothecary, "I am concerned about your cough. It should not linger for weeks as it has. I shall give you garlic syrup and some licorice lozenges. But you must rest."

"Thank you, Mr. Galt," said Mrs. Merriman. "I'll have plenty of time to rest after Christmas. 'Tis such a happy, busy time just now!"

Mr. Galt shook his head. "I fear your cough will turn into something more serious if you do not take care," he said. "Mind you, wrap up well. 'Tis frightfully cold."

"Aye!" said Mrs. Merriman. "The cold cuts straight to my bones!" She coughed as she turned to go. "Come along, Lissie," she said. "Good day, Mr. Galt. I wish you joy of the season!"

Felicity and her mother hurried to the milliner's shop. Usually, Felicity was not very interested in the pretty shop full of finery for ladies and gentlemen. Never before had Felicity paid attention to the feathers and fans, the flowery bonnets, fancy shoes, purses, laces, and trims. But today, Felicity studied the shelves. *Perhaps there is something here that could make my old brown gown beautiful,* she

thought. *Perhaps there is something magic here.*
And then Felicity saw the doll.

The doll was standing on a shelf,
holding a bouquet of tiny silk flowers.
She had black painted hair and rosy pink
cheeks and an excited expression. *Look at
me!* she seemed to say. Felicity stared. The
doll's gown was made of blue silk. It was the bluest
blue there ever was—bluer than the sky, bluer than
the sea—a blue so bright it lit up the shop. The
neck and sleeves of the gown were trimmed with a
frill of lace as white and delicate as snowflakes. It
was the most beautiful gown Felicity had ever seen.

*Oh, if only I could go to the Palace in a gown like
that*, thought Felicity. She was so lost in her
daydream, she was surprised when she felt her
mother's hand on her shoulder. Mother stared at
the beautiful doll. She was caught by the doll's
magic, too.

"Isn't her gown perfect?" sighed Felicity.

"Aye," said Mrs. Merriman. "But you surprise
me, Felicity. I've never known you to care about
gowns and such before!"

"I've never been invited to the Palace before!"

Felicity burst out. "I've never *needed* a beautiful gown before!"

"Ah!" said Mrs. Merriman. "I understand."

The milliner took the doll out of the case and handed it to Felicity with a smile. "I'm quite proud of that gown," she said. "I made it for the doll myself. I copied the pattern from one I saw Lady Dunmore wearing at church. It is the very latest style from England." She held the doll's gown up to Felicity's cheek. "That blue would look lovely with Felicity's pretty red hair, Mrs. Merriman."

"Yes, indeed, it would," said Mother. "But . . ."

"I have the bolt of blue silk right here," said the milliner. "And I have made a lady's-sized pattern for the gown. It would take only a bit of adjusting to make the pattern fit Felicity."

Felicity looked at her mother with a face full of longing.

Suddenly, Mrs. Merriman smiled. "You shall have the beautiful blue gown, Lissie, my dear," she said. "I will make it for you myself."

"Oh, thank you, Mother!" Felicity exclaimed. "Thank you!" She smiled up at her mother and hugged the pretty doll.

"Your father will say I've been foolish," laughed Mother. "But after all, it *is* Christmas. And it's the first gown you've ever *wanted*. Besides, how many times is a young lady invited to the Governor's Palace? We will show everyone in Williamsburg how proud we are of our Lissie. You will look as fashionable as Lady Dunmore herself!"

Quickly, the milliner wrapped the blue silk in a tidy parcel. "I know you are a fine needlewoman, Mrs. Merriman," she said. "But if you have any trouble, do please ask me for help. The finish work may be a bit hard."

Mrs. Merriman looked a little worried. "Oh, dear," she said. She tried to stifle a cough with her handkerchief.

"I'll help you, Mother!" Felicity burst out. "At least, I'll *try*."

Mrs. Merriman handed Felicity the parcel. "We will *both* try," she said. "And the gown will be lovely. You wait and see!"

Felicity was so full of happiness she had no room for words. She held the precious parcel close to her chest and smiled at her mother. *I am going to have the most wonderful gown in all the world*, she thought. *Because I have the most wonderful mother in all the world!*

That very evening, Mrs. Merriman set to work making Felicity's gown. Felicity watched, biting her bottom lip with concern, as her mother cut the slippery blue silk into pieces.

"The pieces are such odd shapes, Mother!" Felicity said nervously. "Will they ever come together to make a gown?"

"I do indeed hope so!" Mrs. Merriman smiled. But she looked a little nervous, too. It seemed like a miracle when she pinned the pieces together and

28

Felicity could see sleeves, a waist, and a neckline taking shape.

The next morning, Mrs. Merriman began sewing the pieces together. Felicity was very eager to help. She threaded the needle for her mother and handed her pins as she needed them. She and Nan stood behind Mother's chair, watching her work.

After a little while, Mother turned to them. "Now, girls," she said. "You are making me uncomfortable. Please don't peer over my shoulders and stare at every stitch I make." Then she smiled. "Wouldn't you rather play with the ark?" she asked.

"Yes!" said the girls.

"Me, too!" said William.

"Very well then," said Mother. "Felicity, you may bring it down."

Felicity stood on a stool to lift the ark down from its high shelf. The ark was a special toy they brought out only at Christmastide. All three children loved to play with the wooden boat and the small painted animals that went inside. Now they sat at Mother's feet, happily lining the animals up in pairs.

Every once in a while, Felicity would pop up to check her mother's progress. "Mother," she said, "must you sew so slowly? Couldn't you make bigger stitches? No one is going to see them."

Mrs. Merriman sighed. "Lissie, you know what I always tell you. Haste makes waste. If you want the gown to be perfect, you must be patient."

Patient! It was *always* hard for Felicity to be patient. It was especially hard now, with Christmas only three days away, and the dance lesson at the Palace just thirteen days after that. But as the next few days went by, Felicity tried very hard to be patient. She stood still for hours while her mother fitted the gown to her. It was quite uncomfortable to stand without moving. But Felicity never complained. And when the fittings were over, she tried to help with household chores so that her mother would have more time to work on the gown. She played with William. She read with Nan. She helped Rose, the cook. Felicity wanted her mother to have as much time as possible.

Because it was the holiday season, friends and visitors came to call every afternoon. In past years, Felicity had enjoyed all the holiday gaiety. She had

fun passing the special Christmas cakes and
listening to the visitors' chatter. But this
year, Felicity was always impatient for
the guests to leave. It seemed to her
that they talked on and on and wasted
time—time when her mother could
have been sewing.

Christmas Eve afternoon brought a steady
stream of guests. Felicity's heart sank every time
she heard another knock on the door, another
hearty voice calling out "Merry Christmas!" She
groaned to herself every time another happy,
laughing group settled in for a long visit. When
the last guests finally left, Felicity sighed with
relief. *"Now* you can work on my gown," she said
to her mother.

Mrs. Merriman coughed. She looked very tired.
"Please, Felicity, don't nag at me," she said. "I have
a great deal of work to do to get ready for
tomorrow. Run along now!"

Felicity did run along. First she went to
Elizabeth's house. Then she and Elizabeth went to
the milliner's shop to visit the pretty doll and study
every detail of her beautiful gown.

31

"Your gown will look like that soon," Elizabeth assured her.

"I hope so," said Felicity. "Mother must still attach the sleeves, and do the hem, and add the lace trim, and—"

"Your gown will be finished in time," said Elizabeth. "Don't worry."

The milliner's doll looked as if *she* hadn't a worry in the world. She smiled at Felicity with a cheery smile, full of hope and bright expectations. Felicity felt happier when she looked at the doll.

As soon as she got home, Felicity ran up the stairs. Carefully, she lifted the unfinished gown out of the clothes press. She held the waist of the gown to her own waist. The blue silk swished down around her feet.

"Humph!" someone snorted behind her. Felicity turned and saw Ben. "That fancy gown!" he scoffed. "That's all you care about. You've become a selfish, foolish girl. You think only of dancing at the Palace in your finery, when you think at all. You don't know what is important anymore. If your horse, Penny, came back now, you'd be too busy dreaming to care!"

*"You've become a selfish, foolish girl," scoffed Ben. "You don't know
what is important anymore."*

"That's not true!" cried Felicity.

"I think it is," said Ben. He turned on his heel and left.

Felicity could not sleep that night. She lay awake thinking about what Ben had said. Was she selfish and foolish? She knew she still loved Penny, the horse she had tamed and then had helped to run away. Couldn't she love dancing and gowns, *too*? She heard some rustling downstairs. She crept out of her bedstead and down the stairs. Felicity saw her mother sitting at the table working on the blue gown by the light of a single candle.

"Mother," whispered Felicity. "Why are you working on the gown *now*? The fire is dying and it's dreadfully cold down here."

Mrs. Merriman coughed a bit and smiled a weary smile. "I didn't have time to sew today," she said. "I was busy with guests all afternoon. Then I had to finish decorating. Tomorrow is Christmas."

Felicity looked around the dark parlor. She could see that her mother had decorated every windowpane with a cheery sprig of holly. "The parlor looks beautiful, Mother," said Felicity. She hugged her mother. "You make *everything* beautiful."

Mrs. Merriman smiled at Felicity as she folded the blue gown with care. "I love the greenery, too," she said. "It keeps my spirits up and helps me hold on to my hopes of spring." She bent to kiss Felicity's forehead. "And now to bed, Lissie. Tomorrow will be a busy day!"

Christmas Day was full of exciting noises. Cannons roared and guns were fired to mark the special day. People called out merry greetings of the season as Felicity and her family walked to church. Felicity shivered with pleasure when organ music filled the church, and everyone's voices soared together as they sang the joyful songs.

Felicity smiled to herself when the minister read the words of the Christmas story:

And the angel said unto them, Fear not:
for behold I bring good tidings of great joy,
which shall be to all people.

The words seemed to be meant especially for Felicity this Christmas. *There,* she thought, *Father is right. Christmas is not a time for anger. It is a time of great joy for all people. The angel said so.*

There was certainly great joy back at the Merrimans' house when everyone sat down to dinner. Felicity's mother and Rose had prepared a tremendous Christmas feast. Mrs. Merriman sat at the head of the table, serving up steaming bowls of soup and making sure everyone's plate was full of venison, ham, and turkey. She herself cut Ben three pieces of mince pie.

"Rest yourself, my dear," said her husband. "You've stuffed us all and barely taken a bite of the fine feast you and Rose made!" But Mrs. Merriman just smiled and handed around a plate of dates and figs to finish off the glorious meal.

Felicity went to bed full of food and full of happiness. She closed the red-checked curtains around her bedstead so that she would be cozy. She could hear the sweet sound of carolers singing outside beneath her window:

Oh, tidings of comfort and joy,
Comfort and joy!
Oh, tidings of comfort and joy!

Felicity decided there had never been a finer Christmas. As she snuggled under her counterpane and drifted off to sleep, she thought about the beautiful blue gown. *Now that Christmas is over,* she said to herself, *Mother will have time to finish it. That was a thought of great comfort and great joy.

GLOOM AND
SHADOWS

When Felicity awoke the next morning, the house seemed too quiet, especially after the jolly noises of the day before. Breakfast was very odd because Mother was not there.

"Mother is overtired," Father explained. "She wore herself out making Christmas merry for all of us. She needs to rest today. But she says she will be up and about tomorrow."

The day passed slowly. A steady, stubborn rain fell. Felicity couldn't remember a time when Mother had stayed in bed all day like this. Several times Felicity opened the door and peered into the darkness of Mother's room. *Surely she'll be better*

38

tomorrow, Felicity thought. *She'll be well enough to sew my gown. The dance lesson is only twelve days away.*

But Mother was not better the next day, nor the day after that. In fact, she was much worse. Coughs shook her frail body. She was burning with fever one minute and shivering with chills the next.

Mr. Galt, the apothecary, came to see her. When he walked out of her room, he shook his head and frowned. "She is very ill, Mr. Merriman," he said. "She is so worn down that she has no strength to fight the fever. She is struggling to breathe. I am afraid it looks very bad."

"What can we do?" asked Mr. Merriman. Felicity had never seen him so worried.

"Someone must be with her all the time, both day and night," said Mr. Galt. "Keep the fire in her room bright and warm. If she wakes, try to give her water or broth. I will leave some medicine for you to give her, too."

"But how long will she be this way?" asked Mr. Merriman. "Can't we do any more to help her?"

Mr. Galt paused on his way out the door. "All we can do is to hope and to pray," he said. "We must hope and pray and wait."

From that moment, Felicity's life changed. It was as if she had walked out of the sunlight and into a land of gloom and shadows, where it was never bright, just gray all the day long. The outside world did not exist. No holiday visitors came to call. Felicity did not go to lessons at Miss Manderly's, or to Elizabeth's house, or to the milliner's shop to visit the pretty doll.

Felicity, who usually found it hard to sit still for more than five minutes, now took turns with her father and Rose, sitting next to her mother's bedside for hours and hours. She didn't want to be anywhere else. When her mother shook with chills, Felicity covered her with blankets. When her mother tossed and turned with fever, Felicity wiped her forehead with a cool cloth dipped in lavender scent. Sometimes her mother woke, but she was too weak to speak. Felicity held a soup plate of broth to her mother's lips and gave her spoonfuls of it. Most of the time, her mother slept a troubled, uncomfortable, restless sleep.

The days between Christmas and New Year's Day blurred into one long twilight. When Felicity thought about the dance lesson at the Palace and the beautiful blue gown, none of it seemed to matter. There was only one thing Felicity wanted now. She wanted Mother to get well.

On New Year's Day, Felicity sat next to her mother's bed listening to her faint breath. "Happy New Year, Mother," she whispered. Her mother did not stir. A cold, cold fear filled Felicity. Her mother's face was white as the moon. When Mother was well, her hands were always busy, always moving, always making things or doing things for others. Now her hands lay still upon the blankets. Felicity lifted one of her mother's hands and held it to her own cheek. "I won't let you die," she whispered. Felicity wished she could pour some of her own warmth and energy into her mother. If only she could make Mother well! If only there were something she could do! But she was helpless. Felicity put her head down on the bedstead and cried.

When Felicity came out of Mother's room, Father was waiting for her. "You have been a great help caring for Mother," said Father. "I have a New Year's Day present for you." He smiled as he

"I won't let you die, Mother," she whispered.

handed Felicity a lumpy package wrapped in paper. "Go on!" he said. "Open it!"

Felicity pulled off the paper and looked at her present. Her heart twisted. It was the pretty doll from the milliner's shop, dressed in the glorious blue gown, holding her pink bouquet. Seeing the doll made Felicity feel sad. It reminded her of all that she was missing. But Felicity knew her father meant well. He had given her the doll out of love. She could not bear to let her father know his present made her unhappy. So she smiled as brightly as she could and then hugged her father. "Thank you, Father," she said. "It was very kind of you to get the doll for me. Thank you very much."

Her father looked pleased. "Go along now and play with the doll for a while," he said. "I'll sit with Mother. You need a rest."

"Thank you, Father," she said again. Felicity carried the doll up to her room. She sat on her bed and held the doll at arm's length. Its happy expression seemed empty-headed and foolish to Felicity now. "I was just as foolish as you," Felicity whispered to the doll. "I thought a lot of silly things were important before Mother was sick. I know better now." She touched the doll's cool, silky gown once, then gently hid the doll under her counterpane. She didn't want to see her anymore.

"Felicity!" cried a familiar voice. It was Elizabeth. She rushed into the room. "How are you? Oh, I have missed you! I do so hope your mother is better. Look, I've brought you a present. It's a blue silk cord to wear around your neck to the dance lesson at the Palace. It will look fine with your gown."

Felicity did not know what to say. She took the blue silk cord from Elizabeth with a sad smile.

"Why, Lissie!" said Elizabeth. "What's the matter?"

"I can't go to the dance lesson at the Palace," Felicity said dully. "My gown cannot be finished in time. And even if it were finished, I wouldn't go. Father needs me to help take care of Mother. Besides, I couldn't possibly feel like dancing when Mother is so ill."

"Lissie!" Elizabeth said fiercely. "You have to go. Your mother would want you to go."

"I don't want to go anymore," said Felicity.

Elizabeth shook her head. "You don't really mean that! Oh, I wish there were something I could do!"

"No one can do anything," said Felicity. She pulled the doll out from under the counterpane.

Elizabeth gasped. "That's the doll from the milliner's shop!"

"Aye," said Felicity. "My father just gave her to me. I want you to take her. It makes me sad to look at her. It makes me feel foolish when I remember all the hopes I had."

Elizabeth gazed at her friend. Her eyes were full of sorry understanding. At last she said slowly, "Very well, Lissie. I'll take the doll. I'll keep her for a while. But I won't let you forget your hopes. Remember what your father said. Christmas is the time for hopes to come true."

"I've only one hope now," said Felicity, "and that is that Mother will get well."

As the long, sad days and nights of the next week passed, it seemed the rain would never stop. Water dripped off the roof and muddied the ground. Bare, rain-wet branches scratched their fingers against the windows. Felicity was glad the doll was gone. She didn't want to think about the dance lesson. She never went to look at her unfinished gown. She knew seeing it would only make her unhappy.

Mother did not get better. When Felicity was not caring for Mother, she played with Nan and William. It was hard to keep them amused when they were trapped inside every day. But they all liked to play with the ark. They never tired of putting the animals in the ark, two by two.

"It feels as if we have had rain for forty days and forty nights, just as in Noah's story," Felicity said one day.

"Lissie," said Nan. "God told Noah to gather his family and save two of every animal. But what happened to the animals and the people Noah couldn't fit into his ark?"

"Well, the earth was covered with water," answered Felicity. "So I suppose they drowned."

"What's drowned?" asked William.

"It's when you are all covered with water, and you can't breathe, and so you die," said Nan. "And

46

when you die, that means you go away to heaven forever and never come back. Isn't that right, Lissie?"

"Yes," said Felicity.

"Is Mother going to die and go away and never come back?" asked William.

"No!" said Felicity fiercely. She took William onto her lap to comfort him. "No," she said again, more gently. "Mother won't die. She will be well again. The rain will stop. All will be fine again, just as it was in the Noah story. Remember? The rain finally stopped. Noah sent a bird out of the ark. The bird came back with a sprig of leaves in its mouth, so Noah knew somewhere there was land."

Felicity broke a little holly leaf off one of the garlands her mother had made. It was stiff and dry, but it was still green. She gave the leaf to William. "Just think how happy Noah must have been to see a green leaf like this," she said. "The leaf showed him that everything would be all right. It gave him hope."

Nan and William looked at Felicity trustingly. *They need me to be brave*, she thought. So she grinned. "Put the leaf in our ark, William," she said. "Then our Noah will be happy, too."

William lifted the roof of the ark and put the leaf inside.

Felicity looked around the parlor. Most of the Christmas decorations were growing dry and brown. "I know what we should do!" she said. "We must pull down all these dying decorations. We'll make new decorations that are fresh and green. That way, when Mother wakes up, the house will look cheery. *We'll* make some New Year's magic for Mother. Won't that be fine?"

"Yes!" said Nan and William, excited for the first time in a long while.

"Good, then!" said Felicity. She pulled a brittle sprig of holly off one of the windows and tossed it onto the fire. "Let's begin!"

THE SEASON FOR SURPRISES

Felicity leaned forward so that the sleet would not sting her face. She'd had a long afternoon of errands and was scurrying home from her last stop at the apothecary shop with more medicine for her mother. She was buried so deep in her hood, she jumped when she heard a coachman call out, "Stand away, missie!"

She stepped back just in time. Muddy-legged horses trotted by, pulling a carriage through a puddle right in front of her. The wheels of the carriage splashed her petticoat with slush. The carriage hastened on, headed toward the Palace. Suddenly Felicity remembered, *Today is January seventh, the day of the dance lesson at the Palace.*

Felicity shivered. She headed home, cold and wet and miserable.

Felicity hung up her cloak and slipped off her muddy shoes. Her father beckoned her into the parlor. "Come here, Felicity," he said softly.

Felicity's heart thudded. "What is it, Father?" she asked. "Is Mother all right?"

Mr. Merriman smiled. "Come see for yourself!" he said.

Felicity looked behind him. "Mother!" she gasped. Mrs. Merriman was propped comfortably in a big chair next to the fire, cocooned in pillows and blankets. Nan, William, and Ben stood around her. She smiled and opened her arms to Felicity.

Felicity ran to her mother and hugged her gently. "Oh, Mother," she said. "Oh, I'm so *glad*." Felicity wanted to stay in the circle of her mother's arms forever.

"The fever is gone," said Father. "Her cough is still bad, and she is very weak. But at last she is starting to get better."

"I am indeed, thanks to you, Lissie, my good nurse," said Mother. Her voice was hoarse but full of happiness. "You've taken good care of me. Father tells me that you've taken good care of William and Nan, too. Thank you, my dear girl."

"We made new decorations for you, Mother," said Nan. "Lissie did most of the work. But William and I helped, too."

"The parlor looks beautiful," said Mrs. Merriman. "It makes me feel better just to see all that lovely, fresh greenery. What a nice surprise! You truly are my Christmas sprites!" She smiled at Felicity. "Perhaps we could all have a cup of chocolate to celebrate."

"Certainly, my dear," said Mr. Merriman.

"I'll make the chocolate!" said Felicity.

"First you must go and change your clothes," said Mr. Merriman. "You are wet through to the skin. We mustn't have *you* fall sick. Go along now."

Felicity hugged her mother once more, then turned and picked up a chamberstick to light her way up the stairs. *Mother is better! Mother is better!* her heart sang. Felicity felt as if her dearest wish had come true. The cold fear that had haunted her melted away into happiness and relief. *Mother is going to be all right! She really and truly will be all right!*

51

When Felicity reached the door of her room, she stopped stock still. She could not believe her eyes. The beautiful blue gown was spread out on her bed, glowing in the light of her candle. Every stitch was perfectly finished. Was it magic?

Felicity touched it to be sure it was real. The blue silk was as smooth and soft as a sigh, but it was very real.

How could this be? Felicity wondered. *Who finished the gown?* Then she noticed the pretty doll in its matching blue gown sitting upon her pillow. The doll's eyes were bright, and she looked even more cheery and pleased with herself than usual. "Elizabeth!" gasped Felicity. Could she have done it? *Oh, Elizabeth, thank you!* Felicity thought.

Carefully, Felicity lifted the gown in her arms and hurried downstairs to the parlor where her family and Ben were still gathered.

Mother sat forward in her chair. "Felicity!" she gasped. "You have your gown! Your heavenly blue gown! Did *you* finish it?"

"No," said Felicity. "Elizabeth must have!" Felicity held the gown against herself and swirled

around. The blue silk glowed in the light of the fire and brightened the parlor. "Isn't it the prettiest gown you've ever seen?"

"Aye," said Mrs. Merriman. "It is."

Mr. Merriman smiled sadly. "I'm so sorry you can't show off your gown as it deserves. I know this is the day of the dance lesson. But I don't know how you can be properly taken to the Palace. Rose isn't home, and I can't leave your mother. You cannot possibly arrive alone. And there is no one else to escort you."

"I understand," said Felicity quietly.

53

A shadow of sadness crossed Mrs. Merriman's face. She reached out to stroke the glorious blue silk of Felicity's gown.

Suddenly Ben spoke up. "I'll do it," he said. "I'll escort Felicity to the Palace."

Felicity stared at Ben. "But, but Ben . . ." she began. "I thought you . . ." She was too confused and happy to go on.

Mr. Merriman laughed and nodded at Ben with a pleased expression. "Good lad!" he said. He turned to Felicity. "You had better hurry and get ready, Lissie, my dear. 'Tis already nearly four."

Ben was halfway out the door. "I'll get the riding chair ready and bring it around to the front," he said.

Mrs. Merriman's cheeks were pink with excitement. "Edward," she said to Mr. Merriman, "please bring a bathing tub and some buckets of hot water in from the kitchen. Lissie must have a bath. William, fetch some of my very best soap and a linen cloth. Nan, bring the hairbrush. Make haste! We must get Lissie ready to go to the Palace."

Before Felicity knew it, she was

scrubbed clean. Her skin glowed pink and smelled of roses. Nan brushed her hair till it was smooth and shiny as copper. As if in a dream, Felicity slipped the blue silk gown over her head. It fit perfectly. Felicity had never felt so beautiful in her life. Her hands shook a little as she tied the blue cord around her neck. Mother studied her with a loving eye. "Nan," she said, "run and fetch one of my best pearl earrings from the case in my drawer."

Nan hurried to her mother's room and was soon back with the earring. Mother fastened the earring on the blue silk cord around Felicity's neck. "There," said Mother, "there." She sank back into the pillows, looking pleased and proud. "Now you look perfect. Off you go."

Felicity gave her mother one last hug, then pulled on her cloak and rushed outside to meet Ben. It was still sleeting, and the roads were rutted and slippery. But Ben hurried Old Bess along and pulled up to the Palace gates in no time.

Felicity held tight to Ben's hand as he helped her down from the riding chair. She felt rather small when she looked up at the tall iron gates in the wall around the Palace. Tonight the gates were open wide. Inside them, a row of lanterns lit the path up to the Palace doors. At the doors, Ben gave her hand a squeeze. "Thank you, Ben," she

whispered. Ben grinned and disappeared behind her.

Felicity held her breath as she was shown into the Palace entry hall by a footman. The entry hall was big and a little scary. The walls and even the ceiling were covered with fierce-looking swords, pistols, and muskets glinting in the candlelight. Another footman took her wet cloak.

On wobbly legs, Felicity walked the length of the ballroom. A very elegant lady and gentleman stood at the far end under huge portraits of the king and queen. Felicity's heart thumped when she realized, *This must be Lord and Lady Dunmore!* She sank into a blue cloud of silk as she made her courtesy. "My lord. My lady," she murmured, just as she and Elizabeth had practiced so many times. "I have the honor to be Miss Felicity Merriman."

"Miss Merriman," said Lady Dunmore. "How charming! We are so glad you have come to join the others. I believe they are about to begin the lesson."

"Thank you," said Felicity as she rose.

The ballroom was a dazzling blue. Felicity's eyes opened wide in amazement. She'd never seen such a huge room in all her life! It was lit with dozens of candles glittering in chandeliers. *Oh, if only Mother could see this,* she thought. The room was full of young gentlemen dressed in bright silk breeches and coats decorated with gold braid and rows of buttons. Young ladies blossomed like flowers in brocades and taffetas, silks and velvets of every color. *Ah, but my gown is the loveliest,* thought Felicity happily.

Felicity looked around the room. At last she caught sight of Elizabeth and hurried toward her. But just as she reached her friend, the music began. Felicity found herself part of a set of dancers. Elizabeth beamed at her, but they had no chance to talk, for they were soon swept into the music and dancing. The dance master called out the dances. Felicity knew she had better pay close attention. She did not want to make any mistakes!

The beautiful blue gown worked its magic. As the dance lesson went on, Felicity felt more and more at ease. She did not trip, or step on anyone's

"Oh, if only Mother could see this," Felicity said to herself.

toes. In fact, she began to enjoy the dances. The blue gown seemed to help her swoop and swirl and stay light on her feet. *Why, dancing is fun!* she thought with surprise.

And when the dancing was over, the young ladies and gentlemen were invited to take refreshments in the supper room. Felicity had never seen such elegant food! There were towers of sweetmeats and sugared fruits. There were plates of cakes and tarts. Bowls of punch and platters of jellies crowded the long table. It all seemed too beautiful to eat. And Felicity was too excited to be hungry. Besides, she couldn't wait to talk to Elizabeth.

"Elizabeth!" she called. She hurried over to her friend through the throng of people. "You did it, didn't you?" She held out her skirts and twirled. "You finished my gown. But *how* ever did you do it?"

Elizabeth smiled and smiled. "My mother did the hardest parts, but I helped her. Even Annabelle helped," she said. "It looks beautiful, doesn't it?" Felicity smoothed the blue silk skirts and looked at

Elizabeth. "How can I thank you and your mother and Annabelle?" she said. "Oh, Elizabeth! You kept hoping even after I had given up. No one ever had a better friend than you!"

"You have another good friend," Elizabeth said with a grin. "Ben helped me. He sneaked the gown out of your house and then back in again."

"Ben?" asked Felicity. "But he thought the gown was foolish. And he thought it was wrong for me to come to the Palace! How did you change his mind?"

Elizabeth shrugged happily. "I just asked him to help."

"Did you ask Ben to escort me here tonight?" asked Felicity.

"No," smiled Elizabeth. "But I am very glad he did!"

"I am, too," sighed Felicity happily. "I am, too."

When the dance lesson was over, the girls said their thank you's and their good-night's. Felicity wrapped herself in her cloak as she stepped outside the Palace. It was as if all the beauty from the ballroom had spilled out into the night. A fine, cool white powdering of snow had come silently, making the world sparkle. Now the clouds were clearing. For the first time in a long time, Felicity could look up at the stars. The moon lit the clouds from behind, so that they were outlined in silver.

Ben was waiting for Felicity outside the Palace gates. She climbed into the riding chair and sat next to him. They rode in silence for a while. Then Felicity said, "Ben, it was kind of you to help Elizabeth. And it was kind of you to escort me to the Palace. What made you change your mind?"

A wonderful smile lit up Ben's face. "You did," he said. "I watched you take care of your mother. I saw how you cheered Nan and William even when all of the things you had hoped for looked impossible. I began to think your father was right. Christmas *is* the time when our hopes for peace and happiness should come true. I wanted to help your hopes come true, too."

"Thank you, Ben," said Felicity. They rode home together in the silvery night.

LOOKING BACK 1·7·7·4

A PEEK INTO
THE PAST

CHRISTMAS IN 1·7·7·4

An evening of conversation, music, and dance often followed a fancy dinner. Notice the plainer clothes of the servant in the background of this British painting of 1730.

The Christmas season in Virginia during Felicity's time was quite different from the Christmas season we celebrate today. But some things, such as going to church and the pleasures of parties, food, and spending time with friends, were the same then as they are now.

Colonists enjoyed good times during the Christmastide of the 1700s. Several days before

Christmas the festivities began, and they lasted for almost three weeks. Friends and relatives gathered together for feasts and talk and fun. Men rose early to go fox hunting on horseback.

People dressed in their fanciest clothes for parties and balls. Some of the wealthier colonists in Virginia had homes large enough for a ballroom, sometimes with a separate stage for musicians. Some of the balls went on for days and days. One Virginia host was unhappy when his guests insisted on going home after being at his party for six days!

A hunting horn.

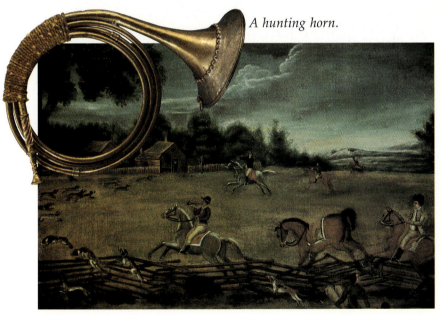

Colonial men enjoyed the sport of fox hunting.

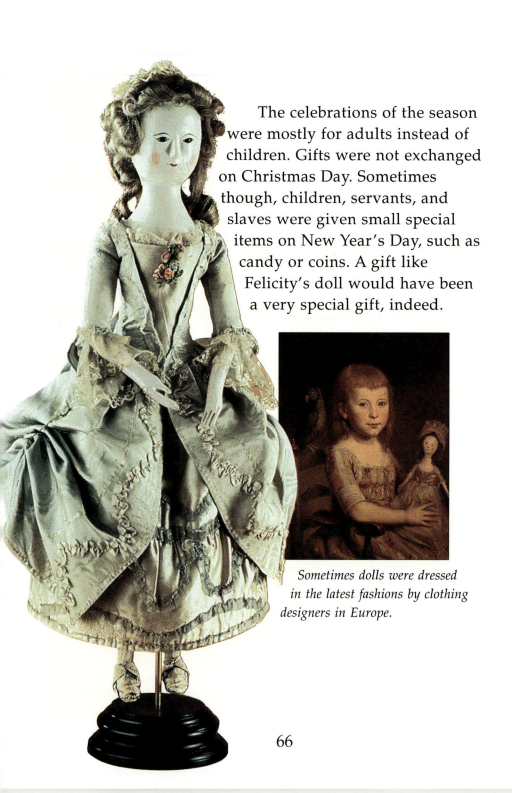

The celebrations of the season were mostly for adults instead of children. Gifts were not exchanged on Christmas Day. Sometimes though, children, servants, and slaves were given small special items on New Year's Day, such as candy or coins. A gift like Felicity's doll would have been a very special gift, indeed.

Sometimes dolls were dressed in the latest fashions by clothing designers in Europe.

A carved set of Noah's Ark figures that belonged to a Pennsylvania family in the 1700s.

Often the men greeted Christmas Day by shooting their muskets into the air. Neighbors heard the sharp crack of the gunfire and answered by doing the same thing. Other neighbors heard those shots and sent the greeting along the way. This custom was called "shooting in the Christmas."

The most important part of Christmas Day was the church service. After church a large feast provided splendid dining. If you had been at Christmas dinner in a home like Felicity's, you might have had turkey, pig, wild birds, oysters, beef, venison, fall vegetables, and plum pudding. In those days, the traditional mince pie was made from chopped meat of many kinds as well as dried fruit.

All of the special meals of the holiday time gave

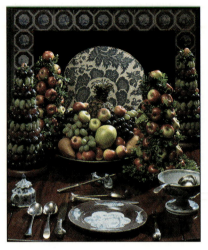

Pyramids of fruit decorated some colonial holiday tables.

colonists an opportunity to show the beauty and order that they valued so highly. Dishes were arranged in lovely patterns on the table to please the eye. The orderly display of large amounts of food on the table was more important to the hostess than how the food tasted. Each course of the meal would often have a spectacular dish that would serve as the centerpiece before it was eaten. And every festive meal ended with men giving formal toasts, sometimes lasting for hours.

The lush greenery of Virginia provided colorful ways to decorate houses. Holly with its bright red berries was a popular choice for many people, like Mrs. Merriman. But colonists picked laurel, ivy, and cedar, too, to decorate their windows and mantels.

This modern picture shows colonial holiday treats of raspberry tarts and glasses with "jelly," a gelatin dessert.

Twelfth Night cakes were often decorated with edible figures made from sugar.

Another practical highlight of Christmastide was the yule log, a giant log that burned for days. This custom was common in England and other European countries. Some people also think that colonists in Virginia burned these giant logs in their hearths throughout the holiday season.

Christmastide ended officially on January 6th, twelve days after Christmas. It was common to have a final party on this day, which was called "Twelfth Night." In some homes, a cake was baked with a bean in it. Whoever found the bean in their piece became king or queen for the day.

The Christmas holidays were not this festive everywhere in colonial America. In New England, many people believed that the holiness of Christmas should be honored, so they had no parties or feasting. But in Virginia during Felicity's day, Christmastide was a time of joyous celebration.

THE AMERICAN GIRLS COLLECTION®

There are more books in The American Girls Collection. They're filled with the adventures that four lively American girls—Felicity, Kirsten, Samantha, and Molly—lived long ago.

But the books are only part of The American Girls Collection—only the beginning. There are lovable dolls—Felicity, Kirsten, Samantha, and Molly dolls— that have beautiful clothes and lots of wonderful accessories. They make these stories of the past come alive today for American girls like you.

To learn about The American Girls Collection, fill out this postcard and mail it to Pleasant Company. We will send you a catalogue about all the books, dolls, dresses, and other delights in The American Girls Collection.

I'm an American girl who loves to get mail.
Please send me a catalogue of The American Girls Collection®:

My name is _____

My address is _____

City _____ State _____ Zip _____

My Birthday is _____ My age is ____

I am in ____ grade.   Parent's Signature _____

The book this postcard is in came from:

☐ a bookstore   ☐ the Pleasant Company Catalogue
☐ a library   ☐ a friend or relative

If the postcard has already been removed from this book and you would like to receive a Pleasant Company catalogue, please send your name and address to:

PLEASANT COMPANY
P.O. Box 497
Middleton, WI 53562-9940
or, call our toll-free number
1-800-845-0005

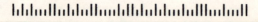